MW00989835

A Vanilla Wife's Guide

Chastity

by Milyssa Morrisette

Contents

Introduction for Men

Let me guess, you are reading this to see if it might help your wife fulfill your dreams of chastity. I think it will, but there's something that you have to do before this can happen.

If you truly want chastity you must put aside all your fantasies, your porn, your wishes and rules.

The only rule when you give her the key is that… well, you have given her the key. She can do or not do what she wants with it. And I promise you, this is what you want. You don't want control. You want to be controlled (or at least this aspect of your life controlled). So give up all your preconceptions, your to-do list for dommes.

You get to be locked up. You hand your wife the key. This is the whole point and all she's signed up for. You don't get to ask for anything more.

You might want the leather and whips, you might want her swinging from the ceiling and howling at the moon, but that's not your decision and the worst way of getting the things you want is to push for them. To insist on controlling her as she "controls" you isn't going to work.

Assuming she's agreed to accept the key to your chastity device all you need to know is that she's in charge. That's in charge of your cock. That's in charge of your sexlife. That's in charge —most of all— with the pacing. If she wants to go farther, that's up to her. Make her as happy as you can each step of the way, at each stage of the kink, and perhaps she'll want to take the next step with you.

But first she has to accept the key. I hope this book will help her or help you convince her. But you have to stop living in the fantasy if you want the reality. If she accepts the key, you must accept the reality.

Introduction for Women

As you can see, this is a guide for vanilla wives. I know the world of chastity is wider than I'm addressing. But I'm not a dominant woman. I'm not a gay man. I'm not a polyamorous swinger with a cattle pen of locked up betas.

I'm a married woman. I love my husband. I like sex as much as the next woman, but I've never been that pushy about this or that, I've never been kinky or even kinky-adjacent.

Men and women are different in their attitudes toward sex. We all know it. Sometimes partners are closer together, sometimes the sex fun comes easy, sometimes it has to be worked at, sometimes you hit deadends. Marriage is hard, but I think it's worth it and worth working to keep it hot, fun, and exciting.

This is what my husband and I did. We've had our ups and downs. We've had times of great sex and dry spells that seemed endless. But we kept at it. After fifteen years of marriage however, we hit a problem.

Our sexlife was suffering. Work, kids, fatigue, and just life in general. Without realizing how, our sexlife became dull, difficult, and barely existent. We realized that we had to start over or at least jumpstart it again.

So I asked him what he thought we needed to do. He then asked me a simple but important question. "What do you want in your sexlife?"

I told him two things:
1. I want verbal affirmations. Compliments, but not just compliments, but just regular, every day "I love you" and other affectionate declarations. I want sexy talk and I want normal talk. I wanted him to openly desire me.
2. I wanted better sex. Not necessarily more frequent (though we weren't great in that department either), I wanted better. I wanted foreplay, I wanted pleasure, and I wanted to cum. I didn't want sex to be a race to the finish line.

It was a simple list. He agreed that he should be doing those things and I agreed to assist him in achieving those things. That meant, I needed to be sexy for him (stay fit, dress nice, etc), I needed to be flirtatious, and I needed to improve my bedroom game as well. I knew this, but I received a surprise when I asked him, "what do you want?"

He then began to explain chastity to me. Where his cock is locked in a cage and I hold the key. There were other things and he wasn't quite sure what he would want, but he was open to pretty much anything that I would be open to.

I was shocked.

If you haven't figured it out yet. I was a vanilla wife. I'm not prudish. I've given a few blowjobs in my day. I've tried plenty of things; some I like, and others that I'm not interested in trying again (anal, spanking). Plus, I'm not much of a porn fan to be honest. I've ready a few smutty books, I enjoy a sexy rom-com, but porn? Not so much. Too sweaty and gross.

So you can imagine my surprise when my husband told me what he wanted was to be dominated and sexually controlled by me. I had no idea that this was something men would want or how to fulfill it.

A little background about my husband. He's a prototypical man. A gruff, beer drinking, sports fan, dude. He was a college athlete, he owns a construction company, he's full of confidence, and had plenty of girlfriends before I came along. After a long conversation and some scary internet research with him, he just wanted me to try this new lifestyle with him.

The main thing he wanted was for me to control our sexlife.

A little background about me. I was a psych major in college. So I wanted to analyze him, breakdown this desire, question his sexual history, inspect his fantasies, and generally try to figure him out. I started to do this, but he wasn't interested in the how or why, he just wanted to come home from a long day's work of being the boss and be told what to do. He said he was tired. Also, I switched to a history major in my third year and ultimately realized I wasn't qualified to be a psychiatrist.

All this to say that, I wanted to do this with him, but I had no idea how. The sources online were helpful only to a point. I couldn't find anything written from my perspective. Much of the advice said that if I wasn't into being the domme then it would never work. Some of it said that some men have an inferiority complex and wanted to be treated like sissies. That wasn't me and that wasn't my husband.

So we had to figure it out on our own (we're still figuring it out, to be honest, but we're getting closer and happier every day). This is what we've settled on. After talking to a lot of men and women online, I've decided to throw this out into the world to see if it's helpful to others because so much of the literature is written from the perspective of a non-vanilla wife.

So I may be a vanilla wife, but I am in charge of my sex life. I cum whenever I want, however I want, and as many times in a row as I want. I lock my husband's cock in a chastity device. I hold the key. Once the bedroom door shuts, I'm in charge and he has to do whatever I ask for with no questions asked.

So if you're a vanilla wife (or married to one), and want to know how to become a Keyholder (or help your wife become one), here's my guide.

1.
Four Types of Vanilla Wives

These are the four basic reactions of Vanilla Wives when it comes to Male Chastity: Nope, Maybe, Okay, Yes.

A "Nope" Wife is not interested in participating in the kink with her husband. A "Maybe" Wife is wanting to know a little more, consider what it will mean and what it will involve before committing, an "Okay" Wife is willing to try it out on a temporary basis, and a "Yes" Wife is happy to try out her husband's kink. We can't all be the "Yes" Wife, but knowing where we fall on this scale will help us move forward. I mean, you're all reading this book, so even if you consider yourself a "Nope" Wife, it means you want to know how to deal with this kink. So let's consider the options.

When your husband tells you that he's into having his cock locked in a cage and asks you to be involved one of these four responses will come to mind, but it's important to realize that your initial response might not be your final response.

I should note that I was probably 80% "Maybe" and 20% "Nope" when my husband revealed his fetish to me, but as I thought about it, I steadily moved into the "Okay" category. Full disclosure, after writing this book, I'm solidly in the "Yes" category, but that still took several years to get there.

So let's look at how each wife proceeds into the kink.

NOPE WIVES

The Nope Wife doesn't want to deal with it. She might not even want to know about it, but that doesn't mean her or her husband are destined for sexual frustration and failure. Here are some things a Nope Wife can do to move forward.

The first thing to recognize is how flattered you should be. Your husband revealed something that was probably a little embarrassing for him to admit and wants you to be at the center of it. That alone shows how much he trusts and respects you. Lucky girl!

The second thing is to realize that the chastity fetish is low maintenance. You get out of it what you put in, but you don't need to put in that much. If you're a Nope Wife, you can tell him that you agree that he should lock up his cock and serve you, but that you don't want to see it or hear about it. Tell him to lock up on his own and place the key in a certain place and go about your life.

But don't forget that his desire is for you to control him, so if you need something done and want to add a little motivation to it, remind him that there's a little key that tells you that he must obey.

And the third thing is that, a little goes a long way. You'll be surprised at how even this little answer will transform him… and you! Perhaps this will assist you into becoming a Maybe Wife, but even if it doesn't, your husband will still have some fun despite your minimal involvement.

Tell him to lock up whenever he feels the need, but that you don't want to hear about it. Make sure the key is placed in a certain place so that you could have access to it if you wanted (just knowing you have access will tantalize him), and —if you want— every now and then invoke the key to gain some authority. Perhaps doing so will cause your thinking to shift…

MAYBE WIVES

You're not totally against the idea or at least you feel like you don't know enough about it to say one way or another. You want to learn more, but not commit to this strange new kink. You're a Maybe Wife.

The first thing you need to do is talk about it. Ask him what he likes about it, what he wants from it (or more accurately: what he *thinks* he wants from it), where he came across such an idea. He might not be able to fully answer or express his urges or put his finger on the origins of it sufficiently for your understanding, but talking about it is the first step.

I realize that not everyone has the capacity for talking about things like I do. My husband hated my tendency to get inquisitive about every bit of information and admission he gave me when we first got together. So ask questions as much as you are comfortable with. I go into more detail in chapter 3.

As a Maybe Wife you're trying to figure out what's holding you back from doing it. Are you embarrassed by the idea? Okay, what can you do to get over it? Or is that a barrier? Perhaps you can use that embarrassment.

I'll be honest, I was embarrassed by it. I didn't understand how to respond so I felt embarrassed. It's a natural response (at least for us Vanilla Wives), but I had to learn to turn it around. You shouldn't be embarrassed, he should. So tell him he's a naughty boy and he should be ashamed of himself.

Perhaps you're turned off by the sight of it. Okay, tell him you don't ever want to see it and you better not catch him touching it either. Set up some penalties for infractions. Perhaps he has to do an extra chore. Perhaps he has to buy you a treat. Chastity is a game, just set the rules and have fun!

Dealing with your objections regarding him is easier. If you see this as an attempt on his part to get out of sex, then demand that one of the terms for being his Queen is that you get to have sex as much as you want. Or perhaps you think he's indulging his laziness by requiring you to do all the sexy stuff. Well, then make sure you work him hard when he's caged up.

He doesn't get to define the chastity relationship. You can taper it to suit your needs and desires. The important thing is to find what's hindering you from enjoying it.

The next thing is set parameters and rules for testing it out. Try it for an hour, for a day, for a night, whatever. Make sure he knows this is an audition. You want to see what it's like, see how he is, see how you feel, etc. There should be a clear starting point and an end point. This takes the pressure off it.

So you're busy identifying the reasons that are holding you back from participating in his kink and you're testing it out. If you discover yourself becoming a Nope Wife and he still dreams of you becoming his Queen, then return to the advice of the first section. I suspect that you'll warm to the idea since it offers us women so many advantages, so assuming he doesn't tire of the idea, then you're reading to become an Okay Wife… (Ouch, I just realized that sounds terrible… You're a wonderful wife, you're a queen!)

OKAY WIVES

So you're okay with the kink and want to explore it. Great! This is where all the fun negotiations come into play, but the temptation is to skip past things and rush into it not knowing what you want out of it. Where the Nope and Maybe Wives might be too slow to proceed, Okay Wives might proceed too quickly.

I go into more detail on this stage in chapter 4.

YES WIVES

If you're a Yes and just want to get a good game plan for what comes next, I cover this part in chapter 5.

However, there's a lot of important material covered in the next two chapters, so don't skip ahead.

But remember, you're a vanilla wife, not a burden or a problem. It's fine to be vanilla. You don't have to like everything. But you're reading this book because you want to move past your comfort levels, you want to try something new. It's a brave thing to do and it's not easy, just be honest about your comfort level. Let your husband know if he's pushing you or you feel like you're going too fast.

Remember: You are the Keyholder.

2.
Four Male Archetypes

So your husband tells you he wants to try chastity. What does that mean?

What kind of man has a chastity fetish?

If you're like me, you knew nothing about male chastity until the man in your life suggested it. When my husband confessed his desire, I didn't know how to respond. It was a little bit scary. So before we talk a little bit more about the kink specifically, I thought we should talk about it generally.

The first thing to note is that it might be more than wanting his dick locked up, but it doesn't have to be. I read tons of testimonials online and there was a wide range of answers for the motivations. There's a whole psychology that I'm not qualified to get into, but it is helpful to know a few basics.

I started seeing four distinct archetypes interested in chastity, which I named the Suitor, the Knight, the Servant, and the Slave.

I list them below because it's easier to frame the kink in these terms. I suspect few men will fit wholly into one single archetype. Most will have a little bit of all of them, but one or two should be more prominent. By understanding these elements it will be easier to be the Queen.

Every man interested in chastity seems to fall into four categories or archetypes. They vary in terms of their moods.

Type	Mood	Description
Suitor	Kinky	Fun loving and into foreplay. Likes fantasy and roleplay.
Knight	Submissive	Obedient, but earning rewards. Happy to please, but wants release.
Servant	Inferior	Wants to be commanded and used.
Slave	Guilty	Wants abuse and insults. Craves humiliation.

The types also have a dominant desire:

Type	Desire	Confidence
Suitor	Pleasure	High
Knight	Duty	Regular
Servant	Control	Low

Slave	Punishment	None

For more on these four archetypes see chapter 9.

By the way, this explains why chastity is becoming so mainstream. It's been the fastest growing kink for a decade, with sales for chastity cages growing exponentially. Not since vibrators has a sex toy so rapidly climbed the popularity charts.

Interestingly, the two segments of the most rapid growth are college aged men and in men mid-40s and above. I can't help but notice that it's the younger men experimenting and the men who are trying to recapture that youthful spark. I'll resist speculating further on what this all means, but my point here is to say that chastity isn't a fringe subculture, but an increasingly common kink. Sorry for that rabbit trail, so let's get back on track.

I recommend spending some time thinking about your husband or, better yet, talking to him, and see what type is most dominant. Maybe have him rate himself using ten points, assigning points for each type he feels himself to be. And you should do it too.

For example, my husband rates himself as 6 Suitor, 3 Knight, 1 Servant, and 0 Slave. That is, he sees himself as dominantly Suitor and Knight, with a little slice of Servant. Personally, I rank him a 4 Suitor, 3 Knight, 2

Servant, 1 Slave. I find that he slides a little lower from the scale when I assume greater power over him.

Remember, this isn't official and if you don't find it helpful or you need to tweak the categories, then do so. Also, some people aren't into playing such games and analyzing themselves like I am (my husband had a hard time with it too, but he plays my games). This is what helped me. I offer it because I think it might help you.

So ask yourself:

Is he more of a **Suitor**, where chastity is a provocative way of spicing things up? Sometimes sex becomes too routine and chastity is like the male version of lingerie. Lock him up and have fun, ladies.

Is he a **Knight** in need of a Queen? Does he just want to submit to a powerful woman? Even if only temporary. Some men, particularly those who give orders all day, just want a mental break. Or some men are more comfortable following orders. They'll happily do anything with a little direction. Lock him up and have fun, ladies.

Does he have the heart of a **Servant**? Does he want to be controlled? Perhaps he has a masturbation problem and this would be a helpful way to get that under control (There's plenty of testimony that chastity helped curb porn problems too). Perhaps it's exciting to obey. Lock him up and have fun, ladies.

Or is he a **Slave**? Does he want punishment? Some men need tough love. For some punishment could be seen as affection. Perhaps that touch of danger and extreme sensations ignites passion. Lock him up and have fun, ladies.

A long talk with your man will help you find out where he's coming from. Knowing these things can assist you in figuring out your role in all of this.

My husband seems to fall closer to the Suitor/Knight department, but judging from the information online, there's quite a bit more Slave in men (at least in the chastity kink), but as Keyholder you get to shape all this. Keep reading to find out how.

3.
The Conversation

So your husband tells you he wants to try chastity. What happens next?

Communication is key. We all know it. This advice isn't a secret. Talk things out.

But here's my experience and what I've seen after investing hours reading testimonial after testimonial. Men want some scary, messed up things.

I'm not judging, but remember, I'm a vanilla wife. I'm allowed to be shocked. Chances are, you are a shocked wife too (why else read a guide for vanilla wives?). So what do us, sweet, not-that-kinky, innocent-ish, wives do when our husbands tell us their extreme, dark, weird kinks?

We talk.

Hopefully they don't dump an entirely new lifestyle on you. Hopefully they'll respect you enough to let you work through things slowly. Hopefully they won't be demanding, disappointed, mean, or dogmatic about it.

I'm not a marriage counsellor. I don't know what to tell you if you aren't interested in what they want or who they are. I can only help you if you are wanting to do more for your husband and wanting more from your husband.

If this is the case, if you are willing to try the kink, let me tell you a huge secret: **You are in CHARGE.** You'll get tired of hearing this, I'm sure, but that's because it's true.

Here's a second secret. He will love even a little bit of his dreams coming true. You don't have to be the leather wearing, whip cracking dominatrix of his dreams. You just have to let him hand you a little key.

It doesn't matter if he wants you to tie him up, make him wear a pony costume, flog him, and call him Sally. You hold the key. You make the rules. And he's going to like it.

I have since discovered that chastity is a wonderful kink for men to have because it fits so well with whatever your kink is (unless your kink is to not have a kink and just have a boring or non-existent sexlife).

I don't mean to make it sound easy. It was hard for me at first. I agonized for a week after my husband confessed his fetish. I did research and was scared and horrified by nearly everything I read. But instead of assuming what he was asking for, I just went back and asked.

And let me remind you, he's a blue collar guy. He's beer and bluejeans guy. He's not eloquent. He's not a gabber. He reads books on war and sports biographies. And it takes him months to read them.

He didn't really know what he wanted outside of the feeling of the cage on his penis and the thought of the key in my possession. Some men have a much better idea of what they want or what they think they want. The only way to find out what exactly is to talk about it.

So I just asked. What did he like? What turned him off? I have some advice on how to do that later. Plus there are plenty of sex questionaires that will give insight into his fantasies (if you really want to go there).

And remember: just to ask doesn't mean you're agreeing to do whatever he wants, but knowing is important. You almost certainly will not want to do all of it. I certainly wasn't interested in doing everything my husband mentioned he liked (or might like or wanted to try). I just wanted to know what he wanted.

When I had a better grasp of the four archetypes that I'll discuss later, he was able to recognize his desires better. When I asked what type of Keyholder he wanted (again, see below), he was able to clarify what he was interested in. It wasn't fast, it wasn't obvious where we were going.

But in the end, I took the key. All I knew was that he wanted me in charge of the key, which meant I was in charge of his penis, which meant I was in charge of his pleasure. I felt like a queen.

A queen is in charge of her queendom. Read on to see what else I discovered about being the Queen.

4.
Planning for Chastity

I just needed a way to begin, but there wasn't a guide to help me. It's not enough to decide to do it and dive in. So here's a loose step by step to help you adjust.

If you're not ready to commit and need a little more information, feel free to skip this chapter and read on. When you're ready come back or if you want to set your mind at ease, seeing how easy it is, read on.

First you have to own a chastity device. There's hundreds of types and an overwhelming number of options. Thankfully, this is one of the things the chastity community has a lot of helpful information on. Google it. I'm a big fan of just buying cheap devices on eBay or Amazon. And you should generally default to smaller tube than you think (sorry fellas, but it's true).

It was helpful to be able to shop for a cage with my husband. We picked one out, a plastic one with a cheap little lock and tiny keys. We also purchased a cute little necklace that could also carry the keys. It was like getting engaged and picking out wedding rings. I was still nervous about this new path, but already it was bringing us together.

Tip 1: Shop for a cage.

Once his cage arrived we had another conversation. How long would he wear it? This is the difference between playing chastity and a lifestyle. Playing chastity makes it an event, like longform foreplay, that will conclude and begin again later. Lifestyle chastity makes it more or less full time.

As to how long, my husband's answer was as long as I wanted him to wear it. It sounded like he wanted to play chastity rather than enter into it full time. But either way, when you're starting out, it's better to start out slow: an hour, then later multiple hours. After a while try for a day, then a night, and then all day and all night. Try it for three days, five days, a week, etc.

Whether playing or lifestyle, there should be times for maintenance unlocking. Cleaning is important and you'd obviously want to remind him of what he's missing (more on that later).

One more caveat is that the cage has to be comfortable and secure enough to be worn, but many of the cheap cages aren't. So in this exploratory stage, keep shopping for a cage that's comfortable and can be worn discreetly for the locking period.

Tip 2: Lifestyle Chastity or Playtime Chastity.

So now that you have a cage and have decided how it will be used (lifestyle or play), you have to decide how to initiate it and set the rules.

For those pursuing the lifestyle the initiation happens once and there's no need to begin again. I suggest you hold off on the lifestyle option until after you've explored the kink thoroughly and he's adjusted to the cage. If lifestyle is the route then make rules regarding showers, swimming, gyms, air travel, etc. Feel free to ask and discuss, but the decision is ultimately yours. It's his fetish and not yours (at least not yet, because I assume you're also a vanilla wife).

My advice is to keep it simple and adjust as you go. Also, I read somewhere about an initiation rite that sounded like great fun. You can do candles and solemn vows, exchange the key, throw champagne on his locked manhood, whatever you want. If it's a new lifestyle you're embarking on, treat it like one.

For those, like my husband, who are more interested in playing chastity, then it becomes a matter of setting the ground rules.

For him the rules are easy: what you say goes. If he doesn't want to play by your rules then he can find another kink.

But you need to work through the when, how, and what of chastity. He can be involved in this discussion, but you're in charge so you make the final call.

It would be a mistake to let the husband decide when to do it and will only lead to frustration because the whole point is to put you in charge and if he has to prompt you then it will only lead to disappointment. I wish someone told me this one. Eventually I figured it out.

Tip 3: Make the Rules.

The When

When? Some do it on the weekends. Some do it each night once they get into bed. Some do it once a month, others twice. I started having him lock every weekend and eventually we added the week I had my period (channelling my inner bitch). Of course, I reserved the right to tell him to cage up on a whim.

And that's it. You don't have to have it all worked out and on a bulletin board, in fact, it's better if he is in the dark about it. All he needs to know is when to put his cage on.

The How

How do you tell him to lock up? You can be the one to lock up him or you can make him do it. I wasn't quite sure how it all fit together, so at first he was the one to lock himself up. It was a secretive thing. He would disappear into the bathroom and come out with a sheepish grin. That didn't work for me, but if that's what you're comfortable with, that's fine. I preferred locking him up, so eventually I made him show me and I learned how to do it.

The point is that he needs to know how it's going to happen.

And then what happens to the key. Does he give it to you to wear? Do you place it on a hook by the front door? You're the Keyholder but that doesn't mean you have to physically hold the key.

My husband nearly died when I accepted the key, dropped it into an envelope and mailed it. Of course, I mailed it to our own house and, of course, I had the backup key (Note: always keep the backup key separate in a secure, perhaps hidden location) but mailing off his key was symbolic. Remember, this is all about control, so make sure he knows how this is supposed to happen.

The What

He doesn't need to know when he's getting out of it or what happens when he gets out of it. You don't even need to know. But you do need to think through what are the things you want to happen, what you're comfortable with.

Before we go into the what in greater detail, let's spell out the Queendom.

5.
Queen of the Queendom

Technically, you're the keyholder. For me this made me feel flush with power, so I began to associate that with being a Queen. I usually equate Keyholder with Queen, but I have some thoughts on the Archetypes of Keyholders below. For now, let's stick with the term Queen.

But first, let me make one small qualification: I don't consider Keyholding to be the same as Femdom. I'm not the boss of my husband. It isn't like a Female Led Marriage, since my control is centered on our sexlife. Outside of it, we were our regular selves, trying to improve our marriage. I didn't feel like a dominatrix and I certainly didn't know how to act like one, but I'd fantasized about being a queen from a very young age. So when I was asked to be a Keyholder it was enough to think of myself as my husband's queen and work from there. Chastity can certainly be a component to Femdom, but the reverse isn't true.

As Queen I needed to know the boundaries of my Queendom. So I divided the world into realms. The Work Realm, the Public Realm, the Home Realm, and the Bedroom Realm. At each realm the Queen's authority grows. At work, since his time, energy, and efforts aren't primarily aimed at the Queen's satisfaction, he is under a lesser authority. In public outings, he could be locked, but I couldn't tell him to bow and kiss my shoes (though I might request he open my car door). At home, I have greater authority. When he's locked, he completes any task or chore I request. But in the bedroom, my authority is absolute. I can tell him to strip, to kneel, to paint my toenails, to dance with me, to dance for me, and to bring me to orgasm until my knees quiver.

We discussed these rules. It was tentative at first as he got comfortable wearing the cage for me and I got comfortable giving him orders. We explored and experimented and the whole time we communicated.

Realm	Rule	Control
Work	Negotiable	Lowest
Public	Whims	Low
Home	Laws	Higher
Bedroom	Absolute	Highest

Description of each Realm

Work: Upon mutual agreement, he could be locked so that his mind and body could be reminded of the Queen's rule all day long.

Public: Within limits of legality and prudence, he could be locked for any outing. All minor whims would be honored.

Home: Under the prescribed agreement, he would fulfill any tasks required of him without question or discussion.

Bedroom: Anything the Queen wants, she gets, without question.

I had a few simple rules. When he's locked, I'm in charge. In between times he's caged, we can discuss and negotiate and even barter, but when I've got the key there's no wiggle room (in more ways than one).

What you will need to do with your husband is discuss how things will work in each Realm. Some might want it to be only a Bedroom thing. Some might want it restricted to the Home and Bedroom. For others all Realms are to be treated as one. Some couples might decide her power is absolute in Public just as it is in the Bedroom. In that case, if she requests that he get on his knees and kiss her shoes in the middle of a restaurant, he will do it. That sort of thing makes me go faint with embarrassment, but if that's what you're into then go for it.

To give an idea of our conversations when he was out of the cage I'll mention a couple of early changes.

Early on, I had no idea that you could sleep in certain cages (some are more comfortable than others, but as always be careful and attentive to your fellow's little fellow). So usually I told him to unlock once bedtime fun was over. He let me know that if I wanted he could sleep in the cage too. So I started having him do that more frequently.

He also mentioned that he could wear the cage outside of the bedroom, if I wanted. So I started telling him to lock up, because, I thought, why not have him thinking about me all day? After a few weeks of me regularly asking him to keep the cage on while at work, he mentioned that it was difficult to do his job while being so distracted. I adjusted to that as well.

I don't want to make it sound like he was telling me what to do. On the other side I was pushing my agenda too. At first, he wanted my Queendom to be restricted to the bedroom. But I thought that if I held the key during the day, that I should wield an appropriate amount of power. That's how I got extra chores out of it. He's a good husband, he helped out with some basic tasks, but now that he was wanting me to be more authoritative in bed, I started using that power in the house as well. Suddenly the garage got cleaned when I suggested it needed cleaning. Suddenly the windows were powersprayed when I mentioned they needed it.

It was really in the Public Realm that I started to explore. I asked that he open my car door when we went out. He did it because it fell into the category of legality and prudence. Had I asked him to strip naked and bark at the moon in the middle of the street, he would've told me that my power doesn't extend that far.

So this made it a fun area of exploration. There's a give and a take to it, but even there he doesn't have full power to decline simply as long as he's in public, because there's also a little thing called Payback. And, as the expression goes, Payback's a Queen (isn't that how it goes?).

For example, at a Christmas party I told him that if I extended my hand to him, I wanted him to take it and kiss my fingers. He politely declined despite being locked with the key around my neck. So that night, in the bedroom, where my power is absolutely, I made him do push-ups until his arms were jelly. Then I told him to shave his pubic hair. He was embarrassed and even a little put out, but I reminded him that he had an opportunity to make me happy earlier.

The next time I asked him to kiss my fingers in public, guess what happened?

In the beginning he said he didn't want it to be a thing just for him, he wanted it to be for me as well. So I made it work for me. I made *him* work for me.

And that's not all that was for me.

6.
What Women Get: Part One

Whatever She Wants.

7.
What Women Get: Part Two

Seriously though, the ability to get some extra work out of my husband wasn't all I gained when I gained the key to his cock.

On top of the benefits of work, I also regained the benefits of romance. Romance hadn't died in my marriage, but it had definitely declined. It is understandable that it declines some after the early part of a relationship (who could ever get anything done with all the kissing and sex?), but I felt that the decline was too steep.

My husband worked hard to make sure things at his business went smoothly and I wanted to adjust things at home to the same level. It wasn't until he confessed the chastity fantasy that I was able to get it.

I made it clear that romance starts first thing in the morning. If he wants something at night, he better start working for it in the morning. I told him I want compliments throughout the day. I want his attention whether I'm present with him or not.

Before chastity, he wasn't as focused on me as I wanted him to be. This is the first great benefit of chastity: nothing focuses a man like taking his sexual pleasure away from him. I call it the Chastity Bump. It's like being newlyweds again. Every touch and glance is meaningful and exciting. My words took on new power and the slighted comment would set him aflame.

I wanted him to be more loving. Once I started locking him up at night, the next morning, when the alarm went off, he would rouse me by kissing my shoulder or brushing my hair gently with his hand.

For the first time in our marriage, I got to shower first, and he would hand me my towel afterwards. I would dress and go downstairs to see that he'd made coffee and sometimes he'd even prepare breakfast.

On some days, my husband's job allows for him to be locked, so I would make him wear the cage all day. I would get texts and messages during the working hours telling me sweet and loving things. Other days I would just tell him that he was going to be locked the moment he got home. Just knowing that he would be in service to the Queen that night was enough to make his imagination enslaved to me.

It became our routine that as soon as he got off work, I would go to the gym and workout and he would either make dinner or clean the house the entire time I was gone. And these weren't little tasks and chores assigned to him under my Queenly authority. These were things he did on his own because he recognized that the happier I was the more I enjoyed my role as Queen. And what made me happy was compliments and a clean house.

This alone would make being his keyholding Queen worth it and that's before we talk about the bedroom stuff. But the benefits to our sexlife were immense.

Before the cage entered our marriage, as I mentioned, the sex wasn't great and wasn't frequent. Maybe once a week. And the routine was set. He would buy me dinner, we'd come home, kiss a little bit, I would suck him to make him hard, we would have sex, missionary or doggie style, he would try to make me have an orgasm first (sometimes I would!), but on times when he popped off first, I would finish myself with my vibrator. He would offer to help, but I was way better at using the vibrator, so I let him fall asleep while I quietly came next to him.

But the cage changed everything.

I'm big into foreplay. I can kiss, cuddle, and fondle for hours. Few things are more enjoyable to me than sitting on the couch, beneath a blanket, drinking wine, watching television, and nuzzling and being nuzzled, touching and being touched, until it's time to get into bed and sweat it all out.

He was big on, well, not that. Get erect and get off was his mantra. We kissed a little, he would pull me out of my clothes, but frequently it was time to be done when I was just warming up to it.

The cage helped me slow things down. My husband can give a wonderful massage when he's in the mood. Sadly, he was rarely in the mood until I started holding his key. Suddenly he would massage my back and feet without complaint. Without asking he would get out moisturizer and slather up his hands, working my back thoroughly and then do my arms and legs. He was so touchy, I was in heaven.

And, yes, the orgasms were amazing. My husband confessed once we started doing chastity that he had never had such an awareness of my pleasure before. I don't mean to imply that he was a bad lover, but once his pleasure was taken off the table, that opened up a whole new world of pleasure for me.

These are the sort of things that really freed me up to enjoy myself. I would tell him, "I want you locked and when I cum three times you can be unlocked for your own fun." Sometimes, if I desired, he would be unlocked the very next day having fulfilled his side of the bargain.Other times I would limit him to giving me only one orgasm a day, but that's the amazing thing. I had to turn down offers of sexual pleasure.

Of course, not every woman wants more sex. I went through times like that too. Somedays I just don't want to be touched. There were times when it felt like my husband was crouched behind every corner waiting to jump my bones. Chastity is perfect for curbing unwanted sexual attention too.

I don't know about the rest of you, but my periods make me irritable and I don't want to be touched. Is that just me? Anyway, I channeled my bitchiness right into his kink. If I don't want to be touched, I lock him up and tell him no touching. He loved it.

So all these advantages can now be yours. I'm telling you, if he's truly into wearing chastity for you, then you will have a husband that will pick up the slack around the house, be more romantic, and give you more sexual pleasure or leave you alone if you want.

This is what you get out of it, but let's look at what he gets out of it.

8.
What Men Get: Part One

Who cares?

9.
What Men Get: Part Two

The thing men most want is to be controlled. I think there are four different types of men who want to be locked in chastity, each with a different need. They might feel equal in all other ways except in the bedroom (Suitor), or feel a sense of duty that they must discharge (Knight), or a more regular pattern of servitude (Servant), or a full time, full bodied devotion to you (Slave).

The thing that ties all four types together is your power. This is the key. Enjoy or abuse it. Now each of these four types will want the same thing in slightly different ways. Determining which type is dominant in your husband will help you know how to treat him.

What they want is the same however. They want to cum. Chastity is a sexual kink. Seems obvious and somewhat counterintuitive. But the end is always to orgasm. Some want it more immediately (the Suitor) than another (the Slave), but every man locked in chastity wants to cum in some manner or other (and it's not always the standard method, but I'm not going into that because I'm a vanilla wife).

They want the same thing, but they want to get there through different means. I've broken it down into three components: Tease, Denial, and Punishment. In the table, I break down the formula (entirely my own), and explain it below.

Here's the formula to approximate how the Keyholder should treat each archetype:

Archetype	Treatment
Suitor	2 parts Tease, 1 part Denial
Knight	50/50 Tease and Denial
Servant	2 parts Denial, 1 part Punishment
Slave	1 part Denial, 2 parts Punishment

Each archetype has a different disposition toward their reward.

Archetype	Orgasm	Reward
Suitor	Full Enjoyment	Deserving
Knight	Controlled Enjoyment	Earned
Servant	Limited Enjoyment	Gift
Slave	No Enjoyment	Undeserving

The Suitor

The Suitor wants sexual pleasure and the cage is just a temporary barrier to it. He's in it for the romance, but he wants to win his prize. For him the time in the cage is a way of testing his resolve. It boosts his arousal state, tempers his impulses, restrains him until it's time to have his way.

For the Suitor, there is little to no punishment because he comes as an equal. He comes for the Keyholder and to win her hand he might have to pass a few trials, but there's no doubt that he deserves the Keyholder. Should there be any punishment it would be minor, an infraction, a slap of the hand, an apology promptly offered.

When he is given his reward it is with open legs or mouth or… whatever. He gets his wild romp in the end. Perhaps he can even make requests while locked up, this is appropriate behavior from the Suitor.

The Knight

The Knight wants to serve, but he'll expect a reward. He's doing noble work and skilled labor deserves greater pay, but he is not an equal, which is why the teasing can be greater and the denial firmer.

Punishment can even enter the equation, though as you'll see below, the scale is quite different. The Knight doesn't want humiliation, but he may be chided and chastised. He might have to make it up to the Keyholder, but he can always regain her favor.

His reward can be earned, but he does not get full right to his pleasure. His pleasure will be measured out accurately. Unlike the Suitor, the Knight does not get anything he wants. His reward will be controlled: a blowjob, a handjob, uncaged sex in the position the Keyholder desires, but there are rules: no touching or no thrusting (or another idea of your own devising).

Devising these rules is part of the fun.

The Servant

The Servant cannot earn his reward. He can be given something, but he cannot earn it. All that he does is what is required. For him the denial goes up and the teasing down. He's well below your station, so there's no playfulness in dealing with the Servant.

Punishment is a regular response to the Servant and the severity increases too. Tasks should be given that cannot be completed in the time required. And embarrassment is definitely on the table. He should be made to feel shame for his failures.

And since he cannot earn rewards, they can be withdrawn at the whim of the Keyholder. Perhaps if he performs the task, he gets to have an orgasm. The "perhaps" should always be offered as a likelihood, but the rewards of a Servant are easily lost. And his rewards should be limited or always contingent on something else. He has five minutes to cum or else he goes back in the cage. Or he may have an orgasm if he can cum by rubbing himself on a pillow. That sort of thing.

The Slave

The Slave is a form of entertainment. Punishment is his constant. Abuse and humiliation are what drives him. Begging is how he interacts. His pleasure should be limited and mostly ignored.

Again, as a Vanilla Wife, there's lots about this end of things that men who are majority Slave (seem to) really enjoy. I'm not into it and since there's abundance of information about this end of things, I don't feel bad by not talking about it in depth. Google, if you're brave, chastity femdom porn to get an idea of what it's about.

One thing I'll add is: remember you are in charge. So much of the porn makes the Slave the center of attention. The way I see it, everything should be focused on the Keyholder. So however you treat the Slave, always remember that you are the focus. That might mean, he's in charge of his own punishments. Maybe send him away and tell him to come back with his bare bottom all shiny and red...

Finally, remember that Punishment is part of control. It doesn't mean you've failed as a Keyholder, it doesn't even mean that you have to be upset that he's being punished. To a degree, punishment is part of the kink. Locking a penis in a cage is going to be uncomfortable and that's what draws people to it. Your punishments are just another element that makes chastity such spicy, sexual fun!

I do want to talk about Punishment, Teasing, Denial, and Ruined Orgasms, but before we get there we need to discuss the Female Archetypes.

10.
Four Keyholder Archetypes

How does a Vanilla Wife become a Keyholder? This was my problem. I'm not dominant in the bedroom. I was very comfortable with my husband playing the lead role. I wasn't exactly submissive either. I don't like taking orders, in the bedroom or out, but having him be in control of sexual activities was my preferred mode.

But now he wanted me to take hold of the key to his cock. He wanted me to treat him differently and I was unsure how to act. Marriage is about compromise, but I didn't know if I could reinvent myself for him.

Luckily, I didn't have to, but I did have to adjust my mindset. What helped me was identifying the four archetypes for the chastity wife. These are the four mentalities that I believe all women have. But just like the male archetypes, a woman might not (and probably does not) fit into one of these exactly. But knowing them, being able to identify your tendencies, will go a long way in helping become a Keyholder.

The four Archetypes are: Nurse, Mistress, Queen, and Goddess. Here's the attitude for each archetype with how they're to relate to their husband. This chart will help you hit the right mindset:

Title	Attitude	Relation
Nurse	Caretaker	Intimate
Mistress	Teacher	Distant
Queen	Master	Superior
Goddess	Divine	Disdain/Remote

And here's a chart for how the archetypes dispense pleasure and pain:

Title	Penalty	Pleasure
Nurse	Correction	Love
Mistress	Discipline	Reward
Queen	Punishment	Temporary Release
Goddess	Cruelty	Denied

It's tempting to align these with the four Archetypes. But don't think that you have to be the Goddess just because your husband identifies himself as the Slave. This is a way of identifying your strengths so that you can channel them more effectively.

Once again use a ten point scale to locate your mindset. I'll be honest, I felt 0 Goddess, 2 points Queen, 3 points

Mistress, and 5 points Nurse. My husband rated me 2 points Goddess, 4 points Queen, 2 points Mistress and Nurse. So I saw myself closer to Nurse and he saw me as closer to Queen. That was helpful in both seeing where he was coming from and helping me identify my strengths.

I see myself as closer to intimate caretaker and he sees me as more powerful. As I began pondering his position, I realized that I frequently dictate questions of clothing, food, and large parts of our schedule. I wasn't necessarily overriding his decisions, he mostly defers to me on such matters, but he registered my actions as Queenly, whereas I saw them as caretaking.

This not only helped me recognize our dynamic, but gave me insight into how to wield the key. But I'm getting ahead of myself. Before going further, let's look at each Archetype in more detail.

Nurse
The Nurse is the caretaker. She's accommodating, but she also knows what's best. Firm, but loving. Chastity for her is about the health of her husband. Making sure he's oriented in the right direction, doing the right things, and also giving him what he needs, whether it's a soft touch or the hard medicine.

In exploring these roles, I had a key phrase that I would say to myself to get into the right mindset. For the nurse I would say, "Poor baby." This would set me in the role.

My husband needed the cage to get himself under control. This is for his own good. I love him and I want him to pleasure me, and this is how we accomplish that.

For some women, this is an easy mindset to fit into. For many men, this is a preferred role, a comforting, loving, and playful partner. Vanilla wives might find it easier to start here and incorporate elements from the other types.

For me, it wasn't a natural fit. I guess I'm just not that nice and my husband isn't a cuddly man. However, I learned that this is the right tone to strike when I'm teasing him or playfully chiding him. When I want to make him feel a little embarrassed, I channel the Nurse, "Does somebody need to be locked up this weekend?"

Mistress

I don't mean mistress as in the side-chick, I mean the female master. Mistress also has her husband's best interest in mind, but there is a greater power dynamic than with the Nurse. She's strict and fair. Her instructions are clear, but they're working together. She has a gameplan or a curriculum that is to be followed. She's flexible though opinionated, and though she has the power to discipline wrongdoing, she will also reward achievements.

My key phrase for the Mistress is, "Now, sir." or "Mr. _____, would you please…" It's a commanding tone that shifts your husband into an attentive and obedient man.

It's just a touch more bossy without being the bitchy boss.

I'm definitely between the Mistress and the Queen. I want things to get done and my husband is in need of being told those things. But I also like to reward. Good boys get treats, is how I think of it. The Mistress is the perfect tone for me because usually after I'm pleasured, I enjoy returning the favor. I'm a nice girl like that. I always give a reward after the hard work.

Queen
The Queen is accustomed to getting what she wants, is firm, but will listen to her underlings. She doesn't reward, because she's getting what she requires, but she will throw in a small bonus every now and then.

The key phrase is, "Yes, ma'am," or "Yes, my queen," and it works best when he's the one saying it. It means he understands his position and your authority. While a Nurse might cajole or convince, and a Mistress might explain, the Queen just tells it like it is. No explanation needed. Plus there's punishment. The Mistress corrects so that the man will do better next time. The Queen punishes because her expectations weren't met.

I had to grow into this role, though at certain times, my mood is definitely that of the Queen. Sometimes, I don't need romance, I don't need cuddles, I just want what I want with no frills, distractions, or to be perfectly honest, no need to reciprocate. I can get what I want and go right to sleep totally guilt free.

Goddess

The goddess is distant from her worshippers. She can go from a little cruel to really cruel. She can be insulting, unforgiving, giving impossible tasks and then dealing out punishments. Being unfair is her divine right.

The key phrase is, "Worm…" The Goddess has unlimited power and no need to show affection. Token gestures of faithfulness are required, bowing, kissing her toes, offering words of devotion…

This is definitely not who I am. So much of the chastity fantasy for men hinges on this sort of dynamic, but ultimately that's a male fantasy because they want to be the center of their wife's sexual attention. They want to be bound and spanked, but while that might be something a wife wants to do, she doesn't have to do any of it. He's the one locked. But having a touch of the Goddess is helpful to add just that extra bit of spiciness. That kick jalapeno or wasabi gives a dish.

Contrary Archetypes

So what happens if your husband's mindset is closer to the Slave and yours is closer to the Nurse? Or if he's the Suitor and you are the Goddess? Remember, you are always the Keyholder, whether your mindset is Nurse or

Goddess. You will always maintain the superior position (at least sexually).

The answer for couples who identify as contrary archetypes is to adjust to the middle.

If he's feeling like a fawning slave, but you feel more loving like a Nurse, adjust to the middle. Treat him as a faithful servant. If his mindset is the Suitor, looking to win the hand of the princess, but you feel godlike and out of his league, then you'll treat him as a princess would treat the advances of an unwanted suitor: kindly dismissive and firm.

These archetypes are to help you think through your actions and responses. Instead of asking "How would a dominant chastity wife handle this?" you just need to ask, "As the Mistress, do I want to do X to my husband?" As the Mistress you maintain distance, but you discipline and reward. How does X fit into that? It's a way of negotiating questions rather than be some ideal dominatrix in your head or, worse, his head, or even worse, in porn.

These four archetypes will help you put a finger on who you are, where your strengths may lie, and how to go about exercising them. And it will assist you in adjusting to various roles as you experiment with chastity. Again, there's no pressure. Explore and discover what you like and dislike, determine what your husband wants and what he needs (which aren't always the same!), and make adjustments accordingly.

Before we move onto the other things, however, I need to make one major clarification.

11.
All That's Necessary

There isn't much you need for a trial run. Chastity is a low maintenance kink. It's a passive kink, meaning you don't have to monitor it. It's like a clock. You set the clock and let it run.

You can obviously do more with it and we'll talk about that below, but at root it requires very few things. All it takes is a man, a keyholder, and a chastity cage. This is all you need to know in order to explore the chastity kink.

So now comes the test period. When my husband got interested enough he bought a cage and wore it secretly for a few months to verify that he would like it and to work out the logistics of it. Once he was sure that this was what he was into, he mentioned it to me. At that point, once I got my head around the idea (which wasn't instant by the way), we decided to test it out.

That's all I agreed to, a trial run, and that's all you have to agree to as well. So before moving on, this is all that a Vanilla Wife needs to do:

- You agree to "hold" the key.

That doesn't mean you have to carry it around or that you are setting times of locking and release. Or that you're going to tease him, humiliate him, dress him up like a maid, or any of that. You just have knowledge that he is locked and the key is yours.

- Determine the Boundaries of the Queendom

No decision is final, but you do need to make some preliminary limits on how long and at what times the cage will be worn during the trial run. Start slow. A make-out session, an hour, and evening.. Also, you need to discuss the powers in each realm: work, public, home, and bedroom. Is this going to be all encompassing powers or just sexual authority?

- Explore his Archetype

Your discussion should begin to probe whether your husband sees himself as the Suitor, the Knight, the Servant, or the Slave. And remember, your opinion matters too. You may see him closer to one than another, more part this than part that. It's important to remember that you're not fitting him into a role. It's more like a recipe. If he feels closer to the Servant, then that gives you insight into what sort of ingredients will go into your chastity play.

- Explore your Archetype

Explore the different mindsets of the Nurse, the Mistress, the Queen, and Goddess. See which type of Queen you want to be. Learn about your strengths and desires and learn about how he responds to these roles. Again, it isn't a role that you're playing. You are finding what mindset helps you.

This is all to get you prepared. He's into the kink to some degree or he wouldn't have mentioned it. This is to allow you to move forward and it also prevents him from dragging you into the role he wants because it pleases him. Chastity isn't about pleasing him, it's about your control. Working through these issues will orient both of you.

A major part of testing out Queendom is knowing the lay of the land. So now it's time to survey it. It's easy.

But to make it even easier, here's a simple, bare minimum option.

Chastity for Beginners

Yes, you'll hold the key.

Designate a place and tell him to put it there.

You want him locked before bed on [Friday] evening.

Chastity is a bedroom event only.

When you tell him to remove the cage that concludes the chastity play until you tell him to put it on again.

While he is locked, discuss the Male Archetypes, this is an opportunity to gauge where he is and what he's into.

Ask about his comfort level, how long he can wear it, where he's comfortable wearing it.

Discuss the Queen archetypes. Tell him how you're most comfortable acting. Give him ideas of the sort of things you'd be interested in receiving and if you're not sure, ask him.

Remind him that his expectations are irrelevant.

This is all pretty simple stuff. It doesn't require leather suits. It doesn't require a psychological overhaul of your personality. Just a cage, a key, and a series of conversations at first.

A Glimpse

Just to give you an idea, I'll give you a glimpse of how it worked for us.

To be honest, despite the conversations and the research and even shopping for a cage, it wasn't until it arrived that I realized he was serious about wearing a chastity device.

I remember the first night once his new cage arrived. I told him to put it on and join me on the couch for a glass of wine. He was so excited that it took him twenty minutes before he joined me. He was wearing his pajama bottoms and a sheepish grin. He took down half his glass of wine in one gulp.

I reached out and touched it through his pants. It was…
different.

And then we talked about it. At the time I asked him how
he wanted me to act. He shrugged his shoulders and
told me that he wanted me to act normal. But HOW? I
kept wondering.

Months later I had a better strategy, but the glass of
wine and the conversation while he was locked up for
the first time was helpful. It was such a special moment.
We bonded. I got to see a new side to him. This is what I
began to appreciate most about being a Keyholder.

It changed our dynamic, but it didn't change who we
were. In fact, I was able to see him far better than
before. I want to talk about this more in the final chapter,
but before we get there I have to address the other stuff.

Don't worry, the rest of this stuff is secondary. As much
as he might want them or fantasize about them, they
aren't the core of the kink. If he truly is interested in the
kink and not just having his own personal little porn
story, then he'll let you set the agenda.

That said, it would be helpful to talk about Punishment,
Humiliation, Tease and Denial, and Ruined Orgasms.

The Inessentials

12.
Punishment

The most important question is, does a Vanilla Wife have to do punishment?

The answer is no. You agreed to hold the key and anything else is optional. But remember the goal to get what you want and that might coincide with what he wants. You first, him second (if at all).

What I wanted was more verbal affirmation and better sex. Being the Keyholder was making him more affectionate, but the question became, how can I improve our lovemaking?

Here's the way I thought about it: if Chastity is about control and delaying orgasm in order to build up to a greater pleasure, then the punishments should add to that too. Remember, this is me getting into the kink. I wasn't a Domme. I still don't feel like a Domme and certainly not if I compare myself to what I've seen in my research.

I want to have fun and enjoy myself as well as give my husband the sort of pleasure he enjoys. If that includes some punishment, so be it. Punishment isn't necessarily expressing my displeasure, but a way of boosting his arousal so that when we did have sex he was primed to give it his all.

Of course, the deeper you go, the more necessary these punishments become. I'll be honest, after getting used to him doing a few extra chores, when he started to slack off on those I resorted to a few of these.

But it wasn't to dominate him (not that there's anything wrong with that, it's just not me). It wasn't to humiliate him (though there's a place for that too). It was to more greatly excite him.

I only mention the types of punishment I'm comfortable with (though we haven't done all of these to be honest). You can supply your own, you can go as far as you want, but this is how I categorize punishment.

PAIN

Spanking
Best: Slaves
Also: Servants
Never: Knights and Suitors
Severity: High to Low
Notes: Highly adjustable, harder to softer, duration, wide choice of rods or paddles. High in the humiliation index.

Personally, I'm not a spanker. We did it a few times as we explored, so I can't offer much advice. For us it wasn't a pure punishment. I had him blindfolded and his palms flat against the wall. I told him I was going to inspect him and that he wasn't allowed to move. I touched, pinched, tickled, kissed, fondled, probed, etc. every part of him and ended with three good spanks on his bare bottom.

Ideas: For the Suitor it should be more off-the-cuff. For the Knight, it should be announced and explained. For the Servant, he doesn't need an explanation, only that you aren't happy with him. For the Slave, no reason need be given, it should only be performed.

Suitor: "I think I need to take you down a notch or two. Please bend over."

Knight: "You didn't respond with the tone I prefer. I think that deserves a spanking."

Servant: "Your behavior is unacceptable."

Slave: "Bend over. I need to get my blood pumping."

Slapping
Best: All
Notes: Highly adjustable in force, from playful to cruel. Can be humiliating, but if lighter then it's teasing.

I've never slapped my husband too hard, though I'll admit to getting more comfortable slapping him. Mostly playful, but if he steps out of line (and he's in more of a Servant mode) then I'll turn his chin.

Ideas: Only performed for the Suitor and Knight in the moment. For Servants and Slaves, the slap can be announced and premeditated.

Icing

Best: All

Notes: Perfect for discouraging an erection. Add a bowl of water for extra chill. Can also double as a humiliation. Sometimes it's necessary for ice to be applied in order to get the cock back into the cage. For the Suitor it's more of a challenge, but the willfulness and intensity increases as you descend the chain of archetypes.

Ideas: From mean request to cruel command. The Suitor and Knight might have more control over the cold, but the Servant and Slave have little to no ability to

Suitor: "I want you to be locked up in ten minutes, so put your cage in the freezer until then."

Knight: "Hold this ice cube against your cage. I want to see how well you handle the cold."

Servant: "I want you to tell me how much you love me while you stick your cage into this bowl of ice."

Slave: "Kneel and dip your cage into that bowl of icy water until I say you can get up."

Hot Wax

Best: Knight
Also: Servant
Never: Slave
Notes: Depending on placement it can be a sharp yet brief pain. It's too intimate and complex for a slave's punishment in my opinion. If it's a feat of endurance then the Knight can undergo this. If cruelly administered it is suitable punishment for a Servant.

I haven't done this one, but if I did, I'd make him clean up any mess.

Ideas: For the Suitor and Knight, the wax can go onto the chest and thighs, but for the Servant and Slave, the more tender areas of the nipples, ass, and even the cage can be dowsed. Restrain Servants and Slaves with rope or handcuffs, but Suitors and Knights get to test their mettle.

Clothes Pins
Best: Servant
Also: Knight
Never: Suitor
Notes: Depending on the placement this could be utter torment or tantalizing stimuli.

Chastity, for those who don't know, increases male sensitivity in other areas. It can widen a man's erogenous zone. My husband wasn't very sensitive in his nipples until a few months of wearing the cage. Now clothes pins are painful for him.

Ideas: The Suitor and even the Knight can be tasked with applying their own clothes pins, but if you decide to do it, you should treat it as a reward, like you're pinning a metal to him. Servants and Slaves can be treated more roughly and dismissively.

Biting
Best: Knight
Also: Suitor
Never: Slave
Notes: Any fleshy place and it only counts if it's too hard. Bite him in passionate throes if he is your Suitor or Knight, or in spite if it's your Servant. Biting seems too intimate for a Slave. The bonus is that you can leave marks.

Scratching/Pinching/Flicking/Squeezing
Best: All
Notes: It needs to break skin if it's a punishment and his back is a perfect spot for your claws. Pinching can be adjusted in strength, duration, and placement. Obviously flicking and squeezing is going to be focused on his scrotum. Even a gentle flick or squeeze conveys a lot to a rowdy husband.

The best part of all of these is that they can (and often do) double as sensual. I know masochists can get excited and aroused by pain, but these mixed into a chastity session will drive any man wild.

Like I said, I was initially resolved to not do anything punishment-wise, you may decide that too. Which is fine. Like I said, you are in charge. But if you find that a little prompting assists you in accomplishing your goals, find what works and use it to your heart's content.

There's another kind of "punishment" that I'll cover in a later chapter, but I'll mention it here. It's actually my favorite method of punishing my husband. It's pleasure; sweet, agonizing pleasure. But before we get to that, we have to talk about one last less comfortable subject.

13.
Humiliation

Humiliation is another motivator. It doesn't have to be mean spirited, it can be light-hearted. But whether you decide to go mean or fun, the end goal is the same: get what you want or turn him on even more (and hopefully both at the same time).

As a Vanilla Wife you might not be comfortable with humiliation (though you might discover that you love it. If so great!). For me, it was another thing that I wasn't into and wasn't comfortable with. I like teasing him some, taking him down a notch even, and embarrassing him a little, but humiliating him isn't a turn on for me.

As with the punishments, try what you want, use what you like, and disregard the rest.

Unlike the punishments, the following Humiliations can be used on all four archetypes. Obviously the will be moderate toward the upper class types (Suitor and Knight) and harsher on the lower class.

There's abundant help online if you want to go deeper/more cruel into this subject. Perhaps you're into it or perhaps he's into it and you want to cater to that desire, but I only want to cover what I'm comfortable with. So if you want a vanilla discussion of this topic, read on.

Bondage
Because of the versatility of this kink, it can be used for all four archetypes. The Suitor and Knight will have more sensual expressions of binding (on the bed, blindfolded), whereas the Servant and Slave would be bound in less comfortable positions (kneeling, closet…).

This can also be used with pleasure or punishment. Suitors loved to be restricted, Knights (because they are fiery like Suitors, but subordinate) require some form of binding. Servants and Slaves should be bound with their wrists behind their back, or wrists tied to ankles, or arms and legs splayed and secured separately. The binding alone is humiliation enough, but other elements can be added.

Stripped
Once again, different types of stripping depending on the archetype you're dealing with. A Suitor or Knight can strip to entertain, remember there's an element of pleasure in your domination of them, but the Servant and Slave should not have an audience while they strip. They're to strip out of your presence and endure the embarrassment of being nude and caged.

I've discovered that men love to be seen in their cage almost as much as they love us to see their penis. The difference is that when they're caged, they're owned.

They love that feeling of being owned as much as that feeling of tightness and restriction the cage provides. Being made to display it on demand adds to their excitement.

Verbal

Verbal Humiliation isn't just insults. It's ultimately a test. For the Suitor it's mild and for the Slave it's intense. You test your Suitor's Desire. How far will he go to win you? You test the Knight's Power. How far will he go to make you happy? You test a Servant's Value. What will he do to serve you? You test a Slave's Obedience. How far will he go to demonstrate your power?

Here's a chart to help you think about how to verbally tease your man (can you tell I like charts?):

Type	Tone	Tease
Suitor	Light	Can't Have Yet
Knight	Edgy	Wish to Have
Servant	Mean	Too Weak to Have
Slave	Cruel	Don't Deserve to Have

Teasing can also come in the form of a threat, but different archetypes require a different touch.

Type	Threat
Suitor	Minor Inconvenience
Knight	Minor Pain
Servant	Major Inconvenience
Slave	Major Pain

Your tone matches the status of the archetype. The source of your teasing is how superior you are and how inferior they are. Think in terms of praising your body and mocking theirs. The Suitor and Knight hear mostly about how great you are and the Servant and Slave hear mostly how pathetic they are.

And obviously the threats depend on their archetype too. The Suitor and Knight get minor threats and the Servant and Slave are taunted by the greater punishments.

Praise: Your Body
Mock: Their Body
Threaten: Inconvenience and Pain at greater or lesser levels (depending on the archetype).

Posing
Posing can be clothed or naked (and every state in between); standing, kneeling, or lying prostrate (or other odd positions). This form of humiliation is also greatly

adjustable depending on the type and the circumstance. Remember to enjoy the Suitor or Knight when undressed and ridicule the Servant or Slave. The more awkward the position, the length required to hold it, and the more exposed, increases the humiliation factor.

To make the Suitor stand attention with his back turned so that you can dress privately is a fit humiliation for the Suitor. To make the Knight or Servant kneel to assist you in putting on your shoes is an excellent idea. To have the Slave stripped naked with his palms against the wall and his head facing the floor is quite appropriate.

Panties
Panties can be used a couple of ways to humiliate. Obviously the first is stuffing your panties into his mouth. It's also a way of shutting him up.

The other use is making him wear a pair. There's a host of reasons for why this is embarrassing. For some it's embarrassing because he's "a big, manly man and delicate things are for ladies." For others it's embarrassing because it accentuates/exposes him (and his cage) in a new and unusual way. For some there's an element of effeminization or sissification that excites him as much as it shames him. Again, I won't go into the psychology of it. Some of it strikes me as sexist, but again, I'm a Vanilla Wife.

I suggest you not think about it. If you think it's funny and it makes your husband blush, go for it. Personally, we haven't done it, but it continues to be a powerful threat. If ever his attention is lagging, my suggestion that he might have to go to work locked up and in a pair of panties usually works in focusing his activities.

Pegging

Vanilla Wife alert! For some this is seen as humiliation, for others this is seen as pleasuring. If I were ever to do it, it would be to give my husband pleasure. (Full Disclosure: EEEEEEEEK!!!) So if you want to know good humiliating pegging tips, please google it. The internet has lots of material that will be explained much better than I can. Sorry! I will talk about pleasurable (or sensual) pegging in the next chapter (OMG, I can't believe I'm going to do that).

In closing let me just say that even in Punishment and Humiliation, ultimately orgasm is the goal. Everything you do is to increase his upcoming orgasm, whether that comes soon after or weeks after (months?). Also, if you don't want to do it, you don't have to. You're the Queen and it's all about what you want.

But you are on this journey because of him so if you think he might enjoy it...

14.
Tease & Denial

I think of Tease and Denial is the inverse of Humiliation. Sometimes a pinch or a smack is how you motivate him or curb bad behavior, bad attitude, or a bad response. Tease and Denial is the carrot, the treat, the boost of encouragement.

It seems odd that taunting him and delaying his pleasure is a positive thing, but remember he is turned on by having the source of his pleasure caged up and his release is in the hands of another.

I don't see Punishment and Humiliation as a critical element to being a Keyholder, but the Tease and Denial is at the center of the kink. Even if all you do is hold the key, there is still the element of denial, but the more you do to draw out his suffering, the more you increase his pleasure and devotion.

If you're naturally flirtatious, then you might not need any help teasing. Simply do what you always do to make him want you. With the cage on, your powers only increase. But for the rest of us, here's a guide to teasing:

There are two parts to Teasing:
- Saying
- Showing

And there are three areas of Teasing:
- Your Power
- His Obedience
- The Cage

SAYING

This means you talk about your power, his obedience, and about the cage. Mentioning those three areas are what will drive him wild.

Examples of things to say:
- I am your Queen.
- You are my Servant/Slave/Toy.
- I control you/ I hold the key.
- You are locked up for me.

The beauty is that while it might help to be explicit (talking about his cock or how he can pleasure you), you don't need to be explicit for it to turn him on. I've never once called my husband "my Manwhore" but I've called him "Mine" and it makes him strain against the cage all the same.

But it's not just you talking about it, making him speak about all three areas will arouse him.

Examples of things to say:
- Tell me I own you.
- Who holds the key?

- Are you my locked man?
- Who is going to massage my feet and kiss my toes tonight?

SHOWING

Also demonstrate your influence in these areas. Making commands to show him your power, so that he can show his obedience.

Examples of commands:
- Get on your knees.
- Go get my hair brush.
- Make me some tea.
- Put on a necktie, cage, and nothing else.
- Take me out to dinner.
- Text me 10 compliments from work.

In person or apart, to get him to tell you how much he loves being owned by you, how he loves to serve you, how he feels having his cock locked up in a cage, those ideas will smolder and flame into deep passion.

Teasing of course isn't restricted to words alone. Obviously trying to arouse him with your clothing and actions is tons of fun (and since he's already primed to be horny, it's an easy win). Dressing sexy, flirting, but also kissing the cage, maybe acting like you're giving him a bj even though he's caged, these are all powerful forms of teasing sure to drive him wild.

And here's a bonus little secret that I'ved discovered. As you no doubt notice, men love their cocks. This holds true for the cages too. I realized that my husband loved for me to see him in his cage, despite the initial embarrassment he felt. But every time I asked him to show it to me, he obliged and then struggled with an erection.

Even now, when I'm the one that puts the cage on for him, I'll still ask to see it a little later.

So tell him to show you the cage when you're together and to send you a picture when you're not.

DENIAL

It's simple, if he's locked, he's denied. The fun comes when you begin to toy with that denial. Your man is water and the cage is the pot. Teasing him raises the temperature of the pot, but the denial is the lid. Bring him to a boil and then shut the lid. Do it right and you get a very satisfying explosion.

Denial is pleasurable torment. He wants to be denied and the game requires you to withhold release otherwise it isn't fun. It's like playing keep-away. You know the game, two people have some item a third person wants and they keep it away from him by tossing it over his head to the other person. That's what chastity is like.

Of course, like any game of keep-away, you have to allow him a chance to get it, but also snatch it away at the last minute. The possibility to "catch it" has to be real, but remember, if it is too easily kept away then the person loses interest in the game.

So denial has to be real, but he has to succeed in acquiring release at some point otherwise the point of the game is forgotten. He wants to cum, but he wants to want it really bad and not get it until he can't stand it any longer.

So how do you achieve that?

There are several games you can play.

He has to give you three orgasms before he can unlock. And remember, you're in charge of when you want an orgasm. I rarely want more than one in a day. Even though my husband would be happy to give me three in a row (at least, now that he's in chastity he does), but I rarely desire it. He just has to wait until I'm ready to earn his release.

Or you can play a dice game. You can purchase sex dice or you can make up your own game. Here's one I made. You can adjust the rules to suit your needs, but here's a template to get you started:

Roll	Result

1	Unlock!
2	Give your Queen an Orgasm if she Wants. If so, unlock. If not: Reroll Tomorrow
3	Kiss the Queen's hand and Reroll.
4	Receive a Punishment (Queen's Choice) and Unlock
5	Do a chore, give a treat or compliment (or all three) and roll again
6	Roll Again Tomorrow

You can also play Key Games. Here are a few ideas:

Key Party
Not that kind of Key Party! No, just put a bunch of keys into a bag and make him earn an opportunity to reach into it without looking and try to find the escape key. You shouldn't use the actual key to his cage because usually they're so distinct from other keys they're easier to find. Even if you find a bunch of keys that look like the actual key, be warned. We've discovered that plenty of keys work in the chastity cage's lock. We designated a special key that feels like the others, but pulling it out of

the bag means he gets to unlock. You can give him ten seconds to keep him from taking too long.

Freezer Burn
Another fun game is to freeze the key. You'll have to suspend it in the water (or else it just sinks to the bottom), but it's a way of making him agonize while it melts. You can let it melt in the fridge for a longer wait, allow him to place it strategically in the house where it might get more sun. My favorite is to make him lick it free.

Hide and Seek
Hide his key and he has to find it. You can do this inside your bedroom, inside house, outside in your yard. We've played a few times where I leave the key in public and he has to find it. First of all, make sure you have a spare key at home, also make sure you leave your phone number on the key in case someone else finds it (remember, you don't have to tell them what it's for only that you dropped it).

I'll be honest, it took me a while before I was comfortable with this one. We started hiding it in the bedroom. I don't know what got into me, but one day I dropped it in the aisle while I was shopping with my husband and then told him he better find it before I checked out. He was breathless by the time he helped me load the groceries, but he'd found the key. It was such a rush that I started going into the store first, hiding it near or under an item that was on his list. Then I'd text him to tell him to come in and begin his search. The best part is that I started giving him most of the shopping list and he still finished before I did.

Randomize
This idea is an easy, low effort way of letting him know when he can unlock. You can say that if the stock market goes up, then he can unlock the next day. Or if his favorite basketball team wins or if they score over 100 points. A few times we've even made bets, such as: "If the first post I see on my facebook account has the letter U in it then you get to unlock tonight. If not it's two more days in the cage."

Be creative but remember to also be **Capricious**. This is an important element to Tease and Denial. You are the Keyholder that means you can make or break the rules. If he pulls out the right key on the first try, snatch it away and tell him to try again. You're playing Keep Away and that doesn't mean it has to be fair. You're bigger, stronger, faster and have all the advantages. Use them as you see fit.

15.
Edging and Ruined Orgasms

There's your pleasure, there's shared pleasure (which is Tease and Denial), and then there's his pleasure. Edging and Ruined Orgasms are definitely his pleasure. If you aren't ready to be involved at this level that's your decision. The order of importance is your pleasure, then shared pleasure, and last is his pleasure.

I repeat: this is optional for you (as is Teasings, Punishment, and Humiliation). However, if you want to enjoy the full powers of the Queendom, then you'll want to add these two things to your bag of tricks.

Edging and Ruined Orgasm are the inverse of Pain. Edging, as I discovered in my early research, is masturbation that stops shy of orgasm. It's a form of torment for your husband, but a pleasurable one.

Edging

Edging is a way of building up desperation and increasing his urgency to obey you. There's also a chemical component to it as well. I won't go into the technical information (Google is your friend, once again), but the shorthand version is that cumming releases the hormones that make him less interested in sex and therefore in you. Keeping him on the edge will keep him attentive and ready to obey.

Also, his orgasms when you do allow him to cum, will be that much more powerful. Seriously, to tease him, edge him, and then satisfy him blows his kneecaps off.

The same principle for Denial still holds true. To delay his release is all part of the fun, but if you go too long it wears him out and erodes trust. For each couple this might be shorter or longer, and certainly you should start slow and build up to longer times as you desire.

Here are some suggestions for Edging.

Obviously, because you are the Keyholder, you don't have to be directly involved. At this point, I promise you, he's really good at stroking himself. You might even learn something watching him. So tell him to edge for ten, twenty, thirty minutes, but not to cum. If he fails, he goes back into the cage and any other punishment you want to add.

To add a layer of difficulty make him edge himself between two pillows. I've heard other suggestions like applying Icy Hot or making him dowse his manhood in cold water after every edge, these are a tad too mean for me, but by all means go for it if you want.

But you can also be involved. You can stroke him while watching television, just make sure you have a codeword for when he gets close to cumming. I like to turn it into a game, see how long I can keep him on the edge before he loses (I'm the Keyholder so I never lose).

You can even edge him while he's in the caged if you have a vibrator. By all accounts, it's intensely pleasurably and a touch agonizing to bring him to the edge by literally rattling his cage.

To be honest, my preferred method of edging him is having sex. It's the best of both worlds. It seems counterintuitive, but chastity improved my access to his penis rather than inaccessible. I was afraid that the cage would lock me away too, but the only change the cage brings is that now you're in charge. So when I want sex, I tell him we're having sex.

What's important is that this sex isn't for him, it's for me. So I make sure I tell him how it happens, faster/slower, this position or that, and I make sure he knows that he's not allowed to cum.

Tell him in advance that he wasn't going to cum and that he was going back into the cage when I was finished him, made him all the more desperate to please me. I've never had him working so hard, but I knew that he was trying to earn his release by special behavior. Normally this would work, I'm a nice girl, but to increase his pleasure means delaying his pleasure. So he goes back into the cage.

Ruined Orgasms

A Ruined Orgasm is when he is brought right up to the brink of cumming and then abruptly stopping. At the right moment his semen will seep out in a sort of soft orgasm that isn't as satisfying and doesn't send him into the refractory period, meaning he can still get hard and cum again.

This is a time consuming process and should be reserved for those special occasions. If he wants to do this on his own, you can certainly allow him to do this, but this is more serving him, than it is serving you. So I consider this a rare event.

Pegging

Like I said above, this is not something I could do, but it's a big enough topic that I should at least address it. Some men have hang-ups and insecurities, but all men have the ability to feel intense pleasure and even achieve orgasm through the stimulation of the prostate. It can be stimulated by a peg (or dildo) or even a hand. There's plenty of resources online to walk someone through the process, but if you think you or he might enjoy it, it would be another way of bringing satisfaction to your caged husband.

Whew. Glad that's over. Now let's talk about the four mentalities you can adopt as a Keyholder.

15.
Beyond Vanilla

I admit that when my husband told me that he was interested in exploring chastity, I was afraid. I was afraid that he was tired of me, that I wasn't enough for him, that I was going to have to be someone entirely different in order to make him happy. And I thought that he would turn into a different person.

My grandfather used to say something when I was growing up: It's hard to be a person. I didn't understand it fully at the time, but I've learned that what he was saying was that people aren't static. They grow, they change, past lives die, metamorphosize, transmogrify, mature, and zig right when life feels like it needs a good zag.

Change is change, but not all change is radical and worldshifting. Change is discovery. Rather than think of the caterpillar as changing into something different, think of it as discovering a new form.

I discovered a new form.

I'm not a dominatrix. My friends tease me that I'm a prude. I don't wear sexy underwear often.

But I tell my husband to lock up his cock. I get what I want in the bedroom. My husband cleans up the bathroom after I have a nice soak and a glass of wine.

I'm not into wearing leather. I don't need kinky fantasies. I never wear heels.

But my husband cums when I say he can. My husband rubs my feet regularly. My husband gets excited when I wear a necklace that has a key.

I'm a vanilla wife. Still. Becoming a Keyholder didn't magically transform me. I have a new form.

I feel like I know my husband better. I know I please him better. And as important, I'm happy too. Chastity for me was a game that I had to learn the rules to before I could fully enjoy.

And like anything, we're still learning and exploring. I don't mean to make it sound easy or give the impression that everything's been smooth sailing since we started this journey, but we're working at it.

I hope this little book helps you explore, eases some of the anxiety, and gives you a way to approach the lifestyle.

APPENDIX

A Template of Rules

Here are some rules I laid down in the early days. I printed off a copy and had him sign it like a contract.

- During the day, the servant may be locked during his time at the office or for chores and errands.
- To begin a teasing session, simply request that the servant lock himself or lay out the symbolic key on his bedside table or send a selfie with the key included in the shot.
- The servant will lock and will not reference his state unless the Keyholder requests verification or initiates teasing.
- The servant may unlock at the conclusion of his work or at the behest of the Keyholder.
- For nightly Chastity, to increase anticipation, it may be indicated beforehand that the servant will be required to lock when evening free time comes. This may be verbal, or a picture indicating his services will be required.
- The Keyholder may request visual confirmation at any time and may physically inspect at any time, but otherwise she need not be concerned with the servant once he is locked.
- When the servant is locked he must give pleasure to the Keyholder in any form she demands, be it fingers, dildo, vibrator or tongue.
- When the servant is locked, the Keyholder may have as many orgasms as she desires.

- At the conclusion of the Keyholder's pleasure, she will inform the servant of the state of his own orgasm. She may determine that he may cum or that he will be teased or denied further.
- If the servant's orgasm is denied, he may remove the cage in a timely manner unless the Keyholder gives specific instructions.
- If the Keyholder decides to tease the servant, once unlocked, she may pleasure and tease him as she desires until she determines whether or not he will cum. The Keyholder may be capricious, granting orgasm at one moment, then revoking it the next. She need not declare the final state of things until the very end.
- The Keyholder determines the method of orgasm as well as the final resting place of the servant's cum. She may stimulate his orgasm herself or request that the servant generate his own, depositing his seed where she desires.

Ten Commandments for Keyholders

1. Control the orgasm, and you control the man.
2. To make chastity work, the Keyholder must Rule without Question.
3. His Stimulation plus His Frustration equals Your Service and Your Pleasure.
4. A Man Testing the Limits of the Rule is a Signal to Reassert the Rule.
5. Denial of Pleasure and Teasing is Equal to Male Satisfaction.
6. The more Aroused a Man is, the more Pleasure he will give.
7. The more effective the Keyholding, the more Pleasure received.
8. All Punishment is a Balance between Intensity and Duration. The More intense it is, the shorter it should be.
9. Submission increases with time. The longer a Keyholder Teases and Denies, the deeper it will go.
10. The Keyholder's control and pleasure are intertwined with the Man's submission and pleasure.

Made in the USA
Columbia, SC
07 March 2022

57338032R00054